Here Comes the SUN

For Ben & Jack
K.N.

For Freddie & Lucia
M.B.

First published in 2017 by Nosy Crow Ltd
The Crow's Nest, 10a Lant Street
London SE1 1QR
www.nosycrow.com

ISBN 978 0 85763 830 4 (HB)
ISBN 978 0 85763 831 1 (PB)

Nosy Crow and associated logos are trademarks and/or registered trademarks of Nosy Crow Ltd.

Text copyright © Karl Newson 2017
Illustrations copyright © Migy Blanco 2017

The right of Karl Newson to be identified as the author and of
Migy Blanco as the illustrator of this work has been asserted.

A CIP catalogue record for this book is available from the British Library.

Printed in China

Papers used by Nosy Crow are made from wood grown in sustainable forests.

1 3 5 7 9 8 6 4 2 (HB)
1 3 5 7 9 8 6 4 2 (PB)

Here Comes the SUN

Karl Newson   Migy Blanco

nosy crow

In a treetop way up high,
Little Owl blinks
and rubs an eye.

Mouse is snoozing,
Squirrel, too.
But Little Owl has work to do.

She spreads her wings, takes off and soon
Little Owl flies up past the moon.

Giraffe is snoozing,
Elephant, too.
But Little Owl has work to do.

Looking for each star that glows,
Little Owl huffs
and puffs and blows.

She blows the stars out
one by one.

But Little Owl's work
has just begun.

Bear is snoozing,
Tiger, too.
But Little Owl has
work to do.

Swooping, looping, left and right,

wishing every star
goodnight.

Whale is snoozing . . .

. . . Penguin, too.
But Little Owl has work to do.

Almost done.
But wait! Oh no!

A shooting star!

Where did it go?

Above the woods
and waterfalls,
Little Owl searches,
Little Owl calls . . .

Over seas and over sands,
jungles,
swamps
and ancient lands.

Goose is stirring,
Camel, too.
But Little Owl has work to do.

Through the night sky, Little Owl flies.

She's tired now,
but then she spies . . .

. . . the very
last
star!

Up and up,
Little Owl goes,

and just in time . . .

...Little Owl blows!

Goodnight, starlight.
Poof! Job done.
The stars are out.

Here comes the sun!

Elk is stirring,
Raccoon, too.
Whale wakes in the deepest blue.

Penguin stretches.
Tigers yawn.
Bear comes out
to meet the dawn.

Elephant sprays.
Giraffe stands tall.

Little Owl says,

"Good morning, all!"

Mouse is waking,
Squirrel, too.
A day is dawning,
bright and **blue**.

Squirrel lifts
his sleepy head,
but Little Owl . . .

. . . flies home
to bed.